The Y̶EAR it all happened

Catherine Bateson grew up in a secondhand bookshop in Brisbane — an ideal childhood for a writer. Her first collection of poetry, *Pomegranates from the Underworld*, was published by Pariah Press. Her second collection, *The Vigilant Heart*, was published in 1998 by University of Queensland Press, and was shortlisted for the John Bray Poetry Award, Adelaide 2000. Catherine now lives in Central Victoria with her husband and their two children. *The Year It All Happened* is a sequel to her first verse novel for young adults, *A Dangerous Girl*.

Poetry

The Vigilant Heart

For Young Adults

A Dangerous Girl

The YEAR it all happened

Catherine Bateson

University of Queensland Press

First published 2001 by University of Queensland Press
Box 6042, St Lucia, Queensland 4067 Australia

www.uqp.uq.edu.au

Typeset by University of Queensland Press
Printed in Australia by McPherson's Printing Group

Distributed in the USA and Canada by
International Specialized Book Services, Inc.,
5824 N. E. Hassalo Street, Portland, Oregon 97213-3640

Australia Council
for the Arts

Thanks to the Literature Fund of the Australia Council for a grant which greatly
assisted the writing of this book.

Cataloguing in Publication Data
National Library of Australia

Bateson, Catherine, 1960–   .
   The year it all happened.

   I. Title. (Series : UQP young adult fiction).

A823.4

ISBN 0 7022 3229 7

For my mother, with love.

Contents

Missing Them

I had it all planned — the best New Year's Eve —
Nick and me, John and Leigh
pulling crackers, pouring champagne,
toasting to our splendid fabulous lives,
our every success in work and love.
Last year it all seemed possible.
Everything was possible.
Until my best friend dumped my brother
and my brother John, drunk and stupid,
gashed his wrist with Grand-dad's old razor.
Now my ex-best friend's gone to Bali,
my brother's gone to Daylesford,
my parents have gone grey,
and if it wasn't for Nick
I'd be lonelier than I can imagine.

I have Nick.
I've made it through to an interview for the course,
my course — Costume Design, Theatre Arts.
There's a bottle of champagne in the fridge,
it's just that half the celebration is missing —
one bit in Bali
the other in Daylesford.
When Nick and I chink our glasses
we're missing that echo.
Missing
them.

JANUARY–FEBRUARY

Daylesford New Year

I spend a week fending off New Year's invitations —
everyone wants me home
except the one person who matters.
She's in Bali with her folks.
She's sipping cocktails in a postcard
she never sends.

Mum and Dad promise a quiet night,
one of Dad's scalding curries,
fireworks on telly and excellent champagne.
Nick and Merri are going in to the city —
real fireworks, jostling crowds.
There are parties until dawn and champagne breakfasts.
I say I'm having a quiet night with new friends,
inventing names on the spot to ease everyone's anxiety.
They don't want a repeat performance —
the clumsy, drunken anguish
spilling blood on the floor of my bungalow.
I don't want a night of forced cheer.
We compromise:
Nick and Merri will drive up New Year's Day
and we'll have a picnic —
so they can see I haven't killed myself.

I'll spend the night in my van, burning candles for her,
playing our last meeting over in my head.
Without Leigh life's a photo from a black and white
    movie —
the girl's always walking away,
her lover watches but she never even looks back.

There's no one to kiss this midnight,
no one who will walk with me into this new year.
The night's as empty as my bed
without her.

The Tree of Hope

Mum says every year's a blank piece of paper
waiting for the next stage of your life to be written
    down.
She burns her failures on New Year's Eve
and writes down wishes to hang in our willow tree
like prayer flags.

I burn my guilt over John and Leigh.
It wasn't my fault she didn't love him enough.
It wasn't my fault he loved her too much.
I tie my wishes next to Mum's.
To get into the Theatre Arts course, Costume Design.
To be with Nick this time next year.
To do my best if I do get in.
To make friends.
To be brave.
I tie one up for John, too.
To find himself.
It stays in the tree the longest of them all.

We hit the road early — the only two people in the world not hung-over. We've got picnic food packed, beer and champagne in the esky, a bag of perfect peaches. Merri's wearing her garden-party hat and I'm wearing my heart on my sleeve. I wish I drove an old ute so Merri could slide over next to me and I could drive all the way to Daylesford with one hand on her bare summer knee.

nick@airspace.com.au — Day-trippers

We pick John up at the lakeside caravan park. He's thinner. I hug him, squeeze his arm. He shows us inside the van — it could be the bungalow moved. Candles, a protea stuck in an empty wine bottle, a lucky river stone and that plan for the catamaran blutacked above the bed. Hey, I say, and punch his arm softly. Hey, Merri says, and lays her head against his shoulder. We have a coffee and start out to a picnic spot called the Cascades. And man, that place is jumping. Everyone's come here today with their left-over champagne, their hangovers and their dogs. We lie around on flat granite slabs like lizards in the sun. We drink, eat, and drink. Kids scramble round the rocks with dogs. Mums call out anxiously about falls, snakes and sunburn. We eat, drink, drink and eat. We talk in short sentences, our mouths full. I fall asleep and when I wake up the sun's dropped and the day-trippers have mostly gone. Merri and John are sitting high up on a rock, shoulder to shoulder. The two people in the world I care about most, deep in sibling conversation.

It can't get any better than this.

After They Leave

The day's too empty.
The night looms ahead,
an open-mouthed whale
ready to gulp me down —
another nightmare journey
into my own misery.
It's all too boring, sitting round
counting your tears
day after day.
Maybe I should go home,
forget this fresh start.
I throw the dice —
four or over I stay,
one to three I pack up.
Six dots stare back, telling me
I've nothing left to lose.

have got me, not the chlorine blue of the pool,
not the postcard perfect ocean blue, but the mean
indigo blues, the black-bruise blues,
the lost and lonely break-your-heart midnight blues.

I thump around the hotel whingeing.
I thump around the pool pouting.
I thump to the markets and don't even bother to haggle.

Finally Marina loses her temper,
calls me an ungrateful bitch and worse.
I'm so bored, I shout, so fucking bored.
And Martin throws his new video camera at me,
Tells me to get out, shoot some holiday footage.
You want to be a journo, don't you? he says,
or an anchor person or whatever?
Start now.
And the M & M's turn their collective back.
He picks up his *Financial Times*
and Mum flips over another page of *Vogue*.
I can't believe what Dad's just handed over
without me even asking — a state of the art toy.
And suddenly everything's green again.
I try a few experimental sweeps of the hotel lobby.
Martin's camera weighs half what the school's did.
Catch my reflection in the lobby mirror
and I have to smile. All I need are shoulder pads
and I could be on the ABC.

What's my story?
Tune in this time next week —
Bali Exposed!
Bye-bye blues.

Leigh's Journal — Sex is just a side order here

'What is it with you guys?' I ask,
and tape the hotel staff confessing to wild sex with the
    visitors.
Older women, they say, with money, cheerfully
    dismissing me.
I meet an Aussie teacher
still here from her holiday in 97.
She tells me about it:
the lazy good sex, the sun, the spiritual sensuality of
    the lifestyle.
She wants to have his baby, bring her up barefooted,
away from grasping consumer capitalism,
the ATM money machine and tupperware values.
How now he wants them to go to Australia.
He wants to live in a brick veneer, Commodore
parked in the double garage, digital surround sound
    telly,
dishwasher hum, shopping mall just a block away.

I'm playing this like I've done it before.
Thesis, I lie, documentary, cross-cultural and gender
    values.
I'm actually interested — and they want to talk, as
    though
no one's stopped to listen to them before.
I don't say much, just nod, touch her shoulder, wink at
    him.

They have more than their fifteen minutes of fame.
They've got a whole tape and they unwind
and let me in everywhere.

I've got more than local colour.
I've got the dirty laundry.

Leigh's Journal — Marina's impressed

with my video. 'Why did they tell you all that?'
she wonders aloud — voicing my question.
'No one's listened before?
You should do something with this.'
She comes back in half an hour.
She has all the details — Short Cuts Across Australia,
a competition for wannabee documentary film-makers,
tv journos, or anyone willing to make a fool of
        themselves
on national television. That's me!
We read through the website pages.
Marina's more excited than me.
She hauls Martin in, makes him promise to help with
        the sound.
It's out of my hands now.
They can hear themselves ringing their friends.
Marina's already rehearsing her smug conversations.
I won't disappoint them — I'm the dutiful daughter.
I send off for the official application form,
tell myself it's better than mooning around,
it'll be something to do before uni starts.
Good practice, that's all.
I try not to get my hopes high.
I watch the video again, pretending to be critical.
It *is* good.
I let myself dream just for one night —
me on tv and everyone watching.

Merri's Interview

I only hear three names — the Head of Department,
Godfrey, 'that's right, darling, God for short'
(I'm too nervous to even twitch a smile),
Edie, Costume Design and History, all chiffon, satin,
    whispery
and Pete, Props Manager, jeans and a tobacco pouch.
They watch me. My portfolio's open in front of Edie.

'Theatre is demanding, a harsh mistress' — Godfrey's
    smooth tones
like the voiceover of a wildlife docco. 'We only want
    blind commitment here.
You must love this theatre,' and he waves an elegant,
    languid hand,
'more than anyone else in your life. Can you do that?'
He's dressed in black, black and black, a silver ankh
    round his neck.
He sounds like Dad after he's had a few, and that makes
    me smile,
tilt my chin up at him and say, just as clearly,
'Yes I can.'
'We expect our techies to also gain stage experience
    and our actors
to paint sets, make props, learn lights and sound. No
    theatre job will be below
your dignity. Not even selling pies at interval. Got that?'
'Yes.'
'Edie? Do you want to say something?

She is your department.'
Edie clears her throat.
'A portfolio exhibiting a certain sophistication
but most importantly for my purposes
a solid knowledge of sewing itself.
I have no time to teach boys and girls to sew a straight
    seam.
I was pleased with your work, Merri. I think you will do
    well.'

I'm in. I'm in.
I fly out of there,
find Nick in the car park, use his mobile to call Mum,
then Dad. Nick calls his mum and we go back to his
    place
for a just-the-two-of-us celebration in bed.

Cleaning out the Bungalow

Half sad, half elated, Nick and I clean out the bungalow
as though we're packing John's life,
his old life,
away. He hasn't left much:
some books, a shirt I thought he loved,
some old best of CDs — just stuff.
And he said I could, last time he phoned.
Sure, he said, clean it out, why not?
Why not? It feels like a betrayal.
'Bullshit,' Nick says, 'he doesn't live here now. That's all.'
I leave his school Shakespeares on the shelf.
I'm on to Romeo and Juliet again — ferals against
        loggers
Juliet with dreads, Romeo in a flannelette shirt.
I believe in tragedy.
I believe in happy endings, too.
Nick and I make love on John's old bed.
It's weird but makes the room my own.
My space with my sewing machine, my books, my clutter.
'Here's to your studio,' Nick says, raising his coffee mug.
And that's it — the room transported — Paris or New
        York —
my *studio*!

O-Week

I collect my show bag,
go to stand in the sausage-sizzle queue,
when I see her:
Leigh. She's wearing cut-offs,
a ribbed cotton top
and a bored expression.
She's fiddling with her hair,
looking round for something,
someone more
interesting to play with.
I dodge out of the queue.
I practically run home,
back to the theatre,
sit panting in the foyer.
I knew she'd be on campus.
I knew I'd see her.
I didn't know she'd still be so vivid
that she'd light up the space around her
like a bright kite in a grey sky.
I didn't know my feet would want to walk over,
my arms already outstretched to hug her shoulders.
I didn't know friendship still hung around this long
after you'd shouted at it to just go away,
to just leave you
alone.

Leigh's Journal — so I go to O-week

big deal — sausage sizzles, free bands and beer
in the courtyard, a show bag complete with condoms.
All the boys have third-degree acne,
all the girls stand round in tight little school groups.
I grab a beer and feel like dancing but no one else is.
The lead singer's cute but the saxophonist is sexy.
Does the sax attract sexy guys or do guys get sexier
playing sax? I down my beer and ask the girl next to me
what she thinks on the subject of saxes and sex.
She smiles, says she has a boyfriend and he's sexy
        enough.

I get up, have another beer quickly and then I dance.
I dance by myself. I dance so well
everyone feels the music sidling into their bones
and slowly, slowly, others come up —
we're doing it together.
I've started a dance revolution.
I tell you, I make things happen when I want to.

Leigh's Journal — Waiting

is the worst thing and I'm bad at it.
Every day I wait to hear from the ABC.
Will they write, email or phone?
Every day I look at their webpage,
hoping not to see a shortlist
without my name.
It doesn't change.
There'll be hundreds of entries.
It could take them weeks.
I read the bio notes of last year's contestants.
They're all in their twenties.
They've all had some kind of film experience.
They all sound confident. They all sound like
winners.

Waiting isn't the worst thing,
losing is the worst thing.
I go back to waiting.

Missing Leigh

In between meeting the caravan crowd
and finding the best swimming spot
I think of her.
How she'd like Tim and his kid, Shayla.
And it's like someone's kicked me in the stomach.
I lose my breath for a minute,
missing Leigh.

In between exploring Daylesford,
the cafes, four bookshops, the hippy clothes shop
just like Brunswick Street, Fitzroy
I think of her.
How she'd pretend to moan about everything being
        green
not concrete grey.
And I have to stop the van,
pull over until I can see again.

At night I dream about her. Sometimes she leaves me.
Sometimes she comes back.
Some mornings I jump out of bed, relieved to be here
in my hot shoebox, in my single bed.
Some mornings I can't get out of bed.
Grief sits on my chest like a boulder.

Missing Leigh.
>Like an ocean with no horizon
>Like a song without a chorus
>Like summer without mangoes
>Like a hole in my heart.
Missing her.

Acrostic for Leigh

Loving her still
Even in the closed face of her indifference.
If she whistled I'd
Go to her, no question —
Heart flapping wildly on my sleeve.

Back jostling for space in the computer lab. Back juggling timetables to get Fridays off. Back drinking bad coffee in the caff. And sitting there for hours with Johnno, Martin and Chao discussing code, politics, assignments and sport. This is how we talk — it's got to be in order — first we deal with technical stuff, then we make a rude comment about the government or America or Bill Gates. Then we catch each other up to speed with assignment stuff. Then we talk about sport. This is the time you can mention any personal problems you might be having. So while we're arguing about who will win this year's grand final, between defending Essendon and bagging St Kilda, I could say, I'm really happy with Merri, you know, but I worry about it being too serious. And Johnno, who barracks for North Melbourne, will put down Essendon and St Kilda with a few choice expletives and then he'll say, yeah, I know girls kind of force it, don't they? Nothing seems enough. I don't reckon Essendon's got a chance, though, Nick, sorry old mate.

I miss John. We talked without rules.

I guess I couldn't talk to him about his sister, though.

Oh well, back to the football!

Merri the Student

Godfrey hauls us all into the theatre — our initiation.
We are to work twenty-four hours a day.
We are to devote our very souls to this theatre.
We will put on two major productions a year
and they will be marvellous.
Anyone who does drugs, sex or suicide in his theatre is
    OUT.
Wait until you're home.
There is one prima donna — Godfrey.
The rest of us are workers.
And we will work.
The boy next to me, Craig,
bleached hair, painted fingernails and yes!
mascara on his eyelashes, whispers
'Yes master,' but very very quietly.
I love it.

I love it from the time I get up and choose what to
    wear.
I even love Voice and Movement with Linda,
six months pregnant and still as elegant as a whippet.
Edie and Costume Design and History are the best.
Edie dresses Alannah Hill meets the twenties in a
    couture junk shop.

She chats about Viv Westwood and Tudor doublets
in the same breathy sentence.
She says everyone must go to the Vic & Albert,

it's wild, she says, Poiret, Vionnet, Erte
and she presses a long-fingered hand to her rib cage.

I have to look up all the names later in the library.
I lug home half a dozen books a day trying to catch up.
Who was Edward Gordon Craig?
Does *Mikado* work in western dress?

And in between all that there's the show.
We're doing *Lysistrata*.
I'm sewing costumes.
I am sewing costumes.

I love this so much I'm almost scared
waiting for something to go wrong.

Whispers in the Foyer

They say each year he picks a third-year student,
girl or boy, sleeps with them, finds them work
on *Home and Away* — he knows the producer.
They say his first wife ran away,
the second's hooked on diet pills.
They say he won't let you cut your hair if you're a
	female actor.
Some girl called Jennifer did one year —
no one knows exactly when —
she'd been a star, the lead of his term-one play,
and then, after the haircut —
they say her hair was down to her waist
and thick as treacle —
mysteriously she failed every subject.
She didn't come back to finish the year.
They say you work all night through, come rehearsal
	time.
Once someone fainted and he didn't even stop,
just left the student lying there until the end.
We whisper in the foyer, the darkest stories,
then Godfrey strides out of his office — Bluebeard
	emerging —
and we jump to attention, pat our hair, sing out hello
in the clearest, innocent voices.

Daylesford

I sit outside my caravan and watch the ducks
on Lake Jubilee. They've got it worked out.
I write lists: each day go for a walk,
each day talk to one new person,
each day lay down another brick
for this new life's foundation.
It's easy on paper.
Take one step at a time, they said.
Don't expect too much. Don't rush yourself.
Man, I'm as rushed as a rainy holiday.
Everything's moving in slow motion
except those blasted ducks.
Bottoms up, heads down, so absurd
I have to laugh and, laughing,
feel suddenly okay.
Add watch ducks to my list.

MARCH–APRIL

Calling Home

Once a week I ring home at the corner pay phone.
Mum always answers first, as though she's hanging
    round the phone.
I make my voice cheerful and I tell her
I've gone swimming every day.

Then I talk to Dad — no, I still don't know what I'm
    doing
but I feel optimistic. I'm slowly meeting new people.
Something will turn up,
something just for me.

Then I talk to Merri.
I ask, casually, if she's heard from Leigh.
There's silence and she says, casually, no but they're
    rehearsing,
she's up to her elbows in Grecian tunics,
they're doing *Lysistrata* —
a bunch of women give up sex to stop a war.
'It's pretty funny,' Merri says, 'big chorus scenes
to give the first years a go on stage.'
'You haven't even seen her
at a distance?'
'Nick sends his love,' Merri says.
She's saying, get over it, John,
but you can't sleep off love
like a hangover.

I've got to move on.
The trouble is I've moved
and my heart has stayed still.

Leigh's Journal — I'm trying to be optimistic

but there just isn't any talent here,
no one I'd waste my smile on.
Half the class is trendy to the max,
the other half tries too hard to be leftie intellectuals.
You can tell the International Socialists by their slogan
     t-shirts,
ripped jeans and dreads. The boys with glasses
all vote Liberal and there's a bunch of greenies up the
     back
who object to photocopied notes and buying
     textbooks —
think of the trees!
I spent four lectures trying to work out who I'd sit with.
Now, I just sit alone. It's safer that way.
I won't catch anyone's pretensions.

Leigh's Journal — I've seen her on campus

and she's always flanked by a couple of loyal friends:
a girl and a gay boy at the very least.
They run round in a little pack.
They all eat together at the Vegie Surprise.
The gay boy has his eyebrows pierced
and his hair colour changes daily.
Sometimes they sit with coffee and hand-sewing.
They don't care who sees them, who smirks.
The journo students call them wankers
and yeah, the actors can be hard to take,
their *darling this* and *darling that*
and the way they never take off those leotards,
but Merri and her friends are just
doing what they want to do, quietly
together.

She never looks up to see me.
She never looks for me.
She doesn't need me.
She's found her own world and I'm at the window,
looking in enviously.

nick@airspace.com.au — My other life

After dark I get on the Net and chat to some friends across the world. There's this dude in Anchorage, Alaska, and we're kind of close. That sounds stupid when I haven't even seen him — except for a fuzzy photo on his homepage — but he speaks my language: we read the same books, watch the same movies, listen to the same music. He's the first person I told when Merri and I got together — apart from Mum. And after John tried to slash his wrists, I emailed Tod and we talked about it. I'd like to go to Anchorage, Alaska, some day and meet my friend.

My mum reckons that's the strangest thing — knowing these people and not knowing them. They could be anyone, she says, you be careful out there, Nick, don't talk to strangers! I'm anyone, too, though — pretended to be a girl once, and this guy wanted to have cybersex with me. I didn't go through with it. Who's interested in cybersex when you can do the real thing with a real girl.

Friends are different. Sometimes it's easier to talk to Tod than anyone else — I don't have to bullshit. Maybe it's because it all happens at night, late, when you're not too worried about the world, when you've had a can or two maybe, when your defences are down and you just start typing fast and press the Send command before your brain realises you've just told the truth to someone you've never really met.

I prise Merri out of the bungalow away from her pencils, inks, watercolours and books. I winkle her out, make her put on her party clothes, set her hair free, kiss the I'm-busy expression from her face. It's a tradition — we always throw a beginning of the semester rage. She'll meet all my friends and colleagues. We'll have fun. I march her to the car. I play loud music all the way there so I can't hear her protests.

It's one of those mad parties. Someone's emptied out a fish aquarium and filled it with the kind of punch that knocks you out slowly. The music's loud and techno. A couple of groovy lecturers are there, furtively chatting up students, or pogoing as though we still do that now.

Merri and I dance, rave, drink too much punch and get giggly. We leave after midnight, lose the car, find it again. The moon's full as a drunkard. I am drunk, too drunk to drive, I decide, after my second attempt to unlock the door. We kiss instead. We kiss and kiss. I know if I stop kissing Merri I'll fall over, so we fall into the back seat instead, kiss until the windows fog. And then my jeans kind of wiggle down and Merri's dress rides up.

That's so sixties, we tell each other, giggling sheepishly afterwards. That's so retro.

And exciting. And we list all the other places we could do it: a study room in the library, the theatre storeroom, the computer lab after closing. I'm still too pissed to drive, so finally we hail a cab and Merri whispers, the backseat of a cab. I laugh too much to tell the driver directions. We get to Merri's and stagger down the back to the bungalow and sleep as close to one another as we can get in the single bed.

Leigh's Journal — It's official, I'm shortlisted

---

one of fourteen. I'm Short Cuts' youngest competitor.
Marina and I danced in the kitchen when the news came.
Martin cracked open a bottle of expensive champagne.
They took me out to the Gilded Egg for dinner.
Everyone's buzzing — photo shoots for all the tv guides,
an in-depth interview with the *Age*.
Triple C want me to say a few words about youth today.
My palms are sweaty, my knees shake
and my head has exploded.

I can't believe I've done it.
There's still more to do — Marina's warning voice.
But I can. I will.
This is it, girl, hang on for the big one!

Leigh's Journal — I've got a filofax

the M & M's congratulations present,
and it is filling up fast: interviews, photo sessions,
appointments, people to see, phone calls to make.
I went to defer my course today but was given a little
    bullshit lecture.
Wait, they cautioned, just see if you do make it.
Hold all decisions.
I nodded and said they were so wise.

Silly fools. I'll make it.
Four intense weeks at the Australian Media School
and then hit the road, jack —
camera and charm in hand.

If I'm one of the lucky ones.
If I'm one of the clever ones.
If — come on, girl —
look at yourself in the mirror.
That's a winner you're seeing.
I hope.

Meeting Ruth

The girl at Dough,
best bakery in town,
leant on the counter today
and asked me my name,
where I came from, and was I looking
for anything in particular.
'Bread', I replied ... 'just a sour dough'.
She meant from life, she said,
she'd seen me walking,
wondered what I was doing in town.
Half an hour later I have her name,
Ruth, her phone number and an invitation
to an anti-logging demonstration.
My van seems bigger when I get back to it,
the lake embraces me like an old friend
when I go for my afternoon dip,
and even the ducks recognise me and waddle up.
I think this is called settling in.
I invite the ducks round for a celebratory sandwich.

Partly Found Poem

Do you want your town to lose
Heritage?
Tourists?
Recreation areas?
Its raw and undeniable beauty?

The Department of Natural Resources
and Environment
is destroying the habitats of natural fauna and flora,
notably
the endangered Powerful Owl.

Call me naive but I just didn't think
the Department of Natural Resources and Environment
was about logging.

Where have you been? Ruth asks,
handing me a placard:
'Out of Wombat State Forest — NOW!'
She's wearing a feathered mask
and a t-shirt splashed with red paint.

We stand outside the MP's office chanting.
A reporter comes and takes our photo —
about fifty of us and a growing petition.
I feel almost like a local!
Especially afterwards at the pub,
backslapping and cheerful,

pots raised and chinked to success.
I've always liked owls. Wise or not
they're magician's birds.
And Ruth, in her own mask,
her dreads like a feathered halo.

Closing Night Party

The set's bumped out by midnight and Godfrey says
    party
at his place. His house is beautiful, predictably.
His wife, serving savouries — not just old cheese
and chips, but cheese platters studded with dried fruit
and a bewildering array of crackers — is beautiful,
    predictably.
There are framed theatre posters on the walls.
The third and second years have seen it before.
They lounge on bright cushions and banana lounges out
    near the pool.
'If this is luxury,' Craig whispers, passing me a smoked
    salmon tartlet,
'Darling, I want it!'
'It's luxury, darlings,' Edie says, slinking up beside us,
holding a glass so heavy her wrists droop, 'enjoy!'
I am. I am. Craig and I tour the house, coveting madly.
Then I get caught up with Tan and the others talking
pregnancies and terminations and suddenly heat washes
    over me
and I have to stand perfectly still.
I haven't had my period. Oh my god.
I've missed it. I haven't even thought of it.
There was so much to do.
Costumes, assignments, costumes.
How late am I?
I find Craig and drag him away from the male chorus
    lead.

'This better be important,' he pouts, 'I was seriously
    tempted.'
I tell him and he shrugs. 'Ducky, it happens all the time:
stress, overwork, a bad cold, a dose of 'flu.
Do you know how hard it is to get pregnant?
I saw a documentary on it once — believe me, those
    wigglers
fight every millimetre of the way. And aren't you and
    Nick
careful? I mean, this is the age of safe sex.'

There was once, I remember, after a party.
It was silly but we couldn't wait
so we did it in the car. I mumble this sheepishly.
Craig laughs so loudly everyone looks.
'What a dark horse you are, Merri.
Look, have a test but don't panic.'

He's right. I have another glass of wine.
I toast the leads, I toast our hosts.
I manage, after all the raised glasses,
to tell Edie how much I love working with her
and am surprised when she blushes and squeezes my
    hand.
I'm home by dawn and then, in the silence of my
    bedroom,
I take off my clothes and look at myself in the mirror.
I couldn't be.
Could I?

MAY–JUNE

Positive

The doctor says
positive.
I have to think about it.
Babies
termination
termination
babies
responsibility
eighteen
Nick and me.
Nick's silent.
He's stone.
Stony.
We get a handful of pamphlets,
her best smile
and a pat for my shoulder.
We get a couple of weeks
to think about it.
It — the baby I'm growing.
The baby Nick and I made.
How can I unmake that?

Haunted

Everywhere I go there are babies:
babies in prams waving their starry hands,
babies being burped, babies in baby backpacks.
Solemn babies looking like the world's a crazy place,
man, and why am I here? Gurgly babies catching the
      sun.
Crying babies. Grizzling babies. Tired babies.
Babies with green snot coming out of their noses.
Babies with crusty eyes and rashes.
Jaundiced babies, babies sicking up thick blobs of
      white glob.
Babies being rocked, joggled, cradled, suckled.
Babies being kissed and handed around — pass the
      parcel.
And that's just at one shopping centre.

I have one too but you can't see her yet.
She's as long as the first two joints of my index finger.
I looked it up in the library. She has eye sockets,
buds for arms and legs and still has a tail.
Not really a baby, not even a foetus.
Don't know if I'll keep this embryo.

Shouldn't have turned the page — by eight weeks
she'll have arms and legs with splayed toes.
She'll have grown eyelids and ears.
She'll be able to hear me say
I hate you,
I love you.

Nick says, what if it's a boy?
I've dreamt her, though. I called her,
she turned, waved and I knew
even in the dark,
I knew her face.

I keep trying to tell Merri it's not that I want her to terminate. I don't know what I want.

What do I know about babies? What do I know about being a father. Only that mine was hopeless at the job, took to drink and bullying and I don't want to be my father's son.

And it's my fault. It's all my fault. So what right do I have to ask for anything?

So I shut up. Nod my head a lot. Agree when I have to.

It's all my fault.

Telling Them

My mother says, ohmygodMerriyoustupidgirl
ohmygodababyadearlittle ...
I mean, I'll support whatever you do.
Dad says, why do you want to make it that hard
for yourself? Do you have any brains up there,
or is it all romantic stuffing?
Mum says, shut up, you're just a man.

Godfrey says, if I hear a baby squeak
during one of my productions
you're out, absolutely, and don't forget the rules
on attendance. I will not accept
morning sickness, feedings, colic, sleepless nights
as an excuse.
Why on earth can't you have a termination
like any sensible girl?

Edie says, we can move a cot into the costume room.
Oh Merri, she says, a theatre baby!

Mum summons statistics to march at her side — teenage mother drop-out statistics, teenage relationship break-up statistics, teenage parenthood fuck-up statistics. She talks about careers. She talks about futures. The grown-up parents nod solemnly.

Merri says, 'I'm having this baby.' She looks straight ahead when she says it. She says, 'I understand your concern but I am having this baby.'

Everyone talks at once. Everyone wants to know if we've thought this through properly. Have we considered where we'll live, what we'll eat and don't think babies aren't expensive. Medical complications, childcare, clothes, schooling. They're talking about schooling and it hasn't even a name yet.

'This will change your lives forever,' Mum says, 'and you can't know that. Are you ready for that?'

'How can they be ready?' Merri's mum sounds cranky. 'Of course they're not ready. I wasn't ready, you weren't ready. No one is ready.'

'My heart is ready,' Merri says.

And that stops all the talk.

First Appointment

The midwives weigh me in, check my urine,
take my blood pressure.
They say, you're at the optimum biological age
to be a mum, but are you happy?
There'll be sacrifices but
you can both grow up together.
They say, it'll be tough for you all,
it's a whole new life but you can make it work.
They show Nick and me round the birthing unit.
It looks like a hotel — if you don't look at the
    equipment.
They make us feel as though we've done something
miraculous.
At the end of the appointment
I don't want to leave.

Dinner at Ruth's

'We'll cruise past the creche' Ruth says, locking up
    Dough,
and pick up Tammy.'
Tammy? Creche?
My mouth hangs open like a hooked fish.
'My daughter,' Ruth said calmly.
'She's four years old.'
Ruth tells me about a country girl, a debutante ball,
a farmer's son and the borrowed ute.

The house is a cottage parked in a field.
There's a dam and Tammy begs for a swim before dinner
'But not nuddy,' she says, 'because he's a boy.'
Ruth shrugs, 'we'll have to go naked,'
she says, 'the boy has no bathers.'
'I'll swim in my jocks,' I promise hastily
and Ruth smiles again
as though she's thinking the world's a funny place
created for her charmed amusement.
'Tammy wins,' Ruth says, 'we'll swim respectably.'

I try not to look at Ruth's singlet and knickers,
her pieced belly button.
I play sharks with Tammy
and don't notice Ruth's breasts,
the soft fuzz under her arms,
her muscular legs.
When we get out Ruth shakes herself,

setting her dreads dancing,
and lets the sunlight pour all over her.
I'm so busy not noticing how beautiful she is
I trip over a log. Ruth helps me up
and I don't let go of her hand
until we're back at the house, in the kitchen,
and then she shakes me gently off.
Hey, I'm so smooth, I'm so cool.
Yeah, smooth as sandpaper,
cool as a High Fire Danger day.
By the third bedtime story Tammy liked me
and even gave me a good night kiss.
Her mother's not so easily wooed —
I'm hugged just long enough to smell her perfume,
patouchli and sandalwood,
before I'm sent dizzily home to my narrow,
restless bed.

Lou Murphy

Ruth takes me down to Murphy's Books
to meet her best friend, Lou Murphy.
I've been there before — but not as Ruth's friend.
Friend? Or possibly more?
I can't tell what Ruth wants.
I don't know yet what I want.

Louise Murphy is in her thirties —
black bob streaked with grey,
bright lipstick and shrewd eyes.
She's a widow and mother of Tammy's
best friend, a precocious dark-haired boy.
He looks as though he's just walked out of Narnia,
with his old-fashioned haircut
and quiet manners.

Lou watches me as we drink coffee
and chat. She watches Ruth.
She watches us together until Ruth gets her going
about her plans for the future.
Lou talks about expanding into bric-a-brac,
affordable old furniture,
doing the auction houses
if she can find someone reliable
who will babysit the shop and sometimes her son, Hugo.
Someone willing to learn about books
rather than just sit behind the counter reading.
I feel my face redden.

I'd do it without pay but I can't tell her now,
not when Ruth, her best friend,
has her hand in a relaxed droop on my shoulder
and I don't know my status here
or what the hell's going on.

When we leave I shake Lou's hand.
I'll come back soon, I promise, telling her in code
not to give my job away!
I walk out of there while Ruth's hand slips
from my shoulder to the top of my waist
where it hangs, companionably, from my belt.
There are signs, portents,
magic in the air.
Only I'm too stupid,
too burned,
to do more than kiss her cheek.
And then lie on my bed for the rest of the night
cursing myself.

Leigh's Journal — We're in hell for four weeks

at the Australian Media School.
The VCE year has nothing on this.
I work round the clock until dots dance in front of my
        eyes.
And still there's my uni work, backing up —
no extensions granted, the bastards.
You'd think they would have been pleased —
the publicity, the hoopla and one of their students.
No, it wasn't like that — congratulations, of course,
said through mouths as pursed as a cat's bum.
And the other students treat me like a pariah.
Jealousy — Marina says sail through, keeping your
        head up.
My head's down, no time to look up!
We're working like slaves.
Everyone's thinner each day.
We snap at each other.
We know seven of us go, seven stay.
We want to be winners, so there's no friendly chat
just cool appraisal. Cnly Mitchell's approachable.
He's such a klutz. We all know — and he says it each
        day —
he'll be out on his arse at the end of the course.
He bumbles around like an oversized puppy.
He gets in the way. And there's Chloe, too —
she's shallow and vain. They'll get rid of her.
You see what I mean? We're not friends here —

someone's bitching about me, that's for sure.
We're cranky and tired, we're suspicious and hostile.
Is this the real world? Is this what it's like?
Grow another skin, girl —
grow armadillo scales!
Well, that was my coffee break —
back to the grindstone,
back to trying to win.

Leigh's Journal — Mitchell's just one of those boys

he can't help himself, trips over his shadow
trying to be mister nice guy — so we've got Friday
     night off
and what does he do? Runs around trying to get us
     together —
pizza and beer at some joint he's found
or a night at the pub and a game of pool.
I'm about to say no, when he tells me everyone else has
     agreed.
I have to study — I'm way behind.
I've an assignment on media law — talk about sawdust,
     dry as.
He has these begging eyes.
It's going to be like sitting in a lifeboat
wondering who goes overboard next.
Come on, he pleads, it won't be the same without you,
     Leigh.
You're so sparky and clever
you get everyone going.
Please?

To say no would be like beating a dog.
I pull on some good trousers, brush my hair.
Remember Marina's business strategy —
making friends with the enemy disarms them.
I smile my girliest smile and watch Mitchell blush.
One down, twelve to go.

T'ai Chi

Jane, the instructor, has quirky eyebrows.
She can almost flick them up,
first one, then the other.
When I tell her I'm pregnant
her eyebrows perform
while the rest of her face remains polished smooth.
When her eyebrows have stopped jitterbugging
Jane says normal things but I know
her eyebrows are curious.
They're wondering how old I am and
if my parents know and whether or not
I have a partner, a drug habit, a good counsellor
and any common sense.
Even while Jane's eyes watch us all
as we stroke the bird's tail
her eyebrows are on me.
I twitch the smallest smile,
giving nothing away.
I like Jane.
It's her eyebrows that worry me.

Juggling

I won't let my dreams slip from my grasp
so soon. I'll juggle all my selves in the air —
flaming torches
and who cares about a burn or two?

Don't keep telling me how young I am —
I know that already.
Don't tell me it will be hard —
I know that already.
Don't keep telling me things I already know.
Tell me something different:
tell me how young women can make great mums,
tell me how young mums can be great students.
Tell me how to get High Distinctions
in all these new subjects I've taken on.

Ultrasound Scan

Nick said he wanted to know the gender of the baby.
I told him she was a girl but he didn't believe me.
The guy doing the ultrasound said the
odds are fifty percent in your favour.
Ha ha, a joke he's told before, I bet.
I lie down, feel like a whale.
Nick holds my hand.
Mum comes rushing in late.
We all hold our breath
and there she is on the screen —
our baby, little hands, little legs,
her head. Mum's crying.
Nick has this goofy grin spread across his face.
The ultrasound guy says,
yep, she's a perfect little lady!
And she lifts one hand,
a victory salute just for me.
I want to wave back,
hello, heart of my heart, I'm here.
Mummy's out here
waiting.

nick@airspace.com.au — Ultrasound Scan

We crowd in beside the bed where Merri's beached. The guy smears jelly on a wand, pushes it down on Merri's bulge and then suddenly there's the baby on the screen. It's real. It's a real baby. I'm really going to be a father. The father of this little thing that's breathing and swimming and really here. I'm so proud.

Love bubbles through me and wants to sparkle out like champagne.

nick@haikuheaven.net.au — Three Poems

Snow in the highlands
and it's still autumn
on the calendar.

Everyone's in coats, scarves, gloves —
Merri just wears a jumper —
the baby keeps her warm.

Branches scrape the roof.
Her back turned to me.
The wind is lonely tonight.

Mothers

You think you finally have everything under control.
No more morning sickness. All your assignments planned
and some even finished. You've been counselled.
You've made decisions about not
making decisions until after the baby is born.
You're organised and feeling good.
Then one morning your mother starts to cry over her
        weetbix.
She's too young to be a grandmother. She's young
        enough to be a mother
all over again if she wanted to be which she doesn't,
thank heavens, or we could be in antenatal class
        together.
She says, look at us, John's off with the ferals in
        Daylesford,
your father's killing himself with overwork,
you're pregnant and I'm going to be a grandmother.
Relax, Mum, we're just a typical dysfunctional nuclear
        family.
She takes to her bed and rings in sick.
I can't understand it. I thought she liked babies.
And she says she does but she's only forty-six.
Get a grip, Mum — I'm the one supposed to be too
        young.
We both are, she says, and cries half the morning.
Should I make her an appointment with my counsellor?
Should I mother my mother?

Getting a Job

I went back to Murphy's Books
alone and told Lou a little more than I wanted to —
about glandular fever and dropping out of school,
about my life being a blank for a few years
or a maze I got lost in. I don't talk about Leigh
and the scar on my wrist.
I don't talk about love at all.
I like this town, I tell her,
and the people, but I need something to do,
something to grow into.

She knows I'm a reader, she's sold me books.
So what? A town with four bookshops
is a reading kind of place.
I sold myself when I talked about wood, my
        grandfather's shed
making furniture, and we were suddenly talking
        together,
planning trips to the auction houses,
a course in French polishing,
stripping back, waxing up, making over,
restoring and transforming.

I've got myself a job, part-time,
flexible hours,
interesting work,
and just because I was there at the right time
sharing a dream.

Moving

It's getting colder in the van.
I pile on another blanket,
put a hot-water bottle at my feet.
Still can't sleep.
My nose feels frostbitten.
Time to move before winter really starts.

I've checked out the noticeboards round town:
Wanted 1 M to share with 2F, 1 M (gay),
must be vegie, have soul
and be house-trained.
Wanted 1 boy to live with 2 wimmin,
three cats and a collection of world music.
Wanted 1 boy symbol, 1 woman symbol
to start enlightened vegan house —
no environment-destroying pets,
children ok.
Wanted creative person to share with a painter,
a muso (drummer) and a nerd (unfortunate).
We're into music, partying and sleepless nights.
If you're a rager, apply now!

I'd be scared of this except Ruth's offered to help.
We'll go into each kitchen with our antennae out.
I want a child-friendly house for Tammy,
a couple-friendly house
just in case.

I want non-smoking, good-eating,
some parties, friendly faces,
a place for my books and my dreams.
I should write a wanted ad
and see how many empty rooms apply.

Settling In

After seeing seven rooms
in six houses,
after eight interviews
in six kitchens, one pub and one café,
after countless phone calls,
and finally, after three firm handshakes,
I find a room I like in a house I like
with people who could become friends.
It's up on one of the Daylesford hills.
There's a veranda and a view,
there's a patch for a vegie garden
and flowers in the front.
My large room faces north
and there's an open fireplace.
I imagine lying in front of it
making love to Ruth.
I imagine her walking out of the shower
dressed only in a towel.
I imagine us eating breakfast together
on the back veranda.
I have a wild imagination.
All that's happened so far
is her hand looped through my belt,
my chaste kiss on her cheek
and one unfathomable look in her eyes
when she didn't think I was watching her.

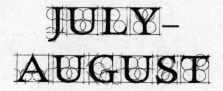

JULY–
AUGUST

Leigh's Journal — After all the pop star hype

the celeb photo shoots,
the radio spot,
the guest appearance on *The Groove*,
I don't make it through.

My mouth's dry as I read the judges' report.
My mouth's dry and my hands are sweaty wet.
The judges found my work lacking in depth,
compassion and a real grasp of what works on
    television.
They thought my work had a superficial sophistication
but lacked real heart.
I need to grow up some more, acquire maturity.
They are sure I will have a future, just not
this year.
The words burn through the paper.
Marina says, 'Leigh, don't lose sight of your achievement.'
She calls me sweetheart.
I let go and cry all over her silk shirt
and she doesn't pull away but tugs me in tighter.

The M & M's are right.
I was the youngest, the least experienced.
I did well.
I did fucking well.
And I won't let the word failure
enter my story.

I'll take this like a professional.
I'll learn and next time
I'll be chosen first.

But for now, I'm having a medicinal tequila
or three.

Leigh's Journal — I can't be sure

but I think Merri's pregnant. I saw her in the library
against a dark window and the light streamed through
    her gauzy dress
shaping the dark bulge, round as a small pumpkin.
And then yesterday I saw her put her hand on her
    stomach
as though she was protecting or reassuring something
    inside.
I looked up the women's body book my mother gave me
— a menstruation present — and Merri must be five
    months pregnant.
She can feel the baby move inside her.
Kicking, the book says, small feet and hands.
I'd like to be the friend who could put her hand
on Merri's stomach and feel that.
If I was Merri's friend, I'd go along to the clinic with
    her.
I'd buy it little clothes. I'd learn to knit.
Not that I want one of my own, understand.
Just that it's such a great big adventure
everything else must feel small beside it —
you can't fail having a baby and
you'd never be alone again.

Leigh's Journal — Failed, failed, failed

that's what this year's been so far.
Failed to get on Short Cuts
and have to watch that Mitchell every week
getting the audience ratings.
There's something about his goofy self-effacement,
the stories that zoom in on him as though he's a magnet
for pathetic bravery: the last truck stop café
between Woop Woop and the Black Stump
closing down due to illness and the capitalist cold
     shoulder,
the teen mum of two in some stupid town
made local mum of the year and Mitch teary-eyed
as he feeds the toddler. Where does he get these losers
     from?
Even that cool director-guy with his trendy goatee
     loves Mitchell.
Every week I rub my own nose in it
— he was the one I pegged to fail.
I was supposed to be the golden girl and look at me —
hauled in now to the Media Faculty at the Batman
     University of Technology,
commonly called BUT and that's what it is — arse-end
     of the world —
to explain my failing two of the three prerequisite units
     for my course.
I was busy?
I was out of town on business?
I was trying a short cut to fame and money,

you hopeless jerks.
Okay, so I failed that too, but I gave it a go.
I gave it a go.

I have to get my second chance.
I'm taking a leaf out of bumbly old Mitch's book.
I borrow a long plain skirt from Marina
and Martin's wool vest — the only surprise being it's
        galah pink.
I knot my hair on my head and I look fantastic;
serious stuff, all I lack are little frameless glasses.
Move over, Lois Lane!
I'm getting this year back
if it means eating an entire humble-pie.
I'll murmur sorry, sorry, sorry and then dazzle them
with my industry experience, my grit and purpose,
my sheer fucking hunger.
I'll get this year back.

Leigh's Journal — What a laugh

Confronted the head honcho, the top gun,
flanked by my two lecturers and one by one
they fell, skittled by all my persuasive charm.
Strike to me.
Actually they were pretty cool after the obligatory rant:
compulsory attendance — for a reason
deadlines on assignments — for a reason
participation in tutorials — for a reason.
Blows I parried with my own:
grasped the opportunity — for a reason
didn't defer — for a reason
realised I must have looked like an arrogant, ambitious
    bitch
for a good reason. But think of it this way
(in my best wheedling tone),
my industry experience is off the slate.
I've done a hands-on four-week course,
Documentary Writing, Editing and Production,
hundreds apply for and only a handful manage.
At my age, I said, a downcast look at my young fingers
obediently twined in my lap, you'd have to admit
some achievement?
I'm allowed a reassessment
first week back of semester two.
Holidays? What holidays?
I'd nothing planned.
And no one to do it with.

Growing

It happens slowly.
First my favourite jeans
the zip stops just short.
Then my black skirt
pops a strained button.
My bras feel tight.
Catch my reflection in the library window —
there's this bulge now —
it's true, then,
I'm growing a baby in there.
Before I go to sleep at night
I place my hands over my belly
and stroke it.
Who cares if you've got nothing to wear
when inside you, still secretly furled
like a new leaf,
there's a baby
waiting for her birthday.

Craig

Craig, the second eldest of six,
says it's all about fluids.
Fluids go in and they come out
of all orifices. In between gurgles.
He makes babies sound like a plumbing problem.
He pats the bump and calls her Tallulah
after some cokehead filmstar.
When I had morning sickness
he brought me water crackers to eat in class.
He's knitting the baby tangerine leggings
to go with a striped velour top he made himself.
Everything looks doll-sized.
Babies are small, he says, but don't buy triple 0,
they grow out of them too fast.
Craig knows all about this stuff.
He'd made a great dad.
Do you want kids? I ask, sort of forgetting
that he's gay. He raises his eyebrows and gives me that
hello is there someone there? kind of look
before offering to babysit
anytime.

nick@airspace.com.au — Where Am I?

Merri and the baby, the baby and Merri. Everyone wants to make the right decision for Merri-and-the-baby, the baby-and-Merri. Where am I in all this? I'm only the father.

Merri decides:
we're too young to get married.
Merri decides:
we can't afford to live together.
Merri decides:
she'll live at home, at least until the baby's born.
Merri decides:
we're a contemporary couple dealing with reality in
    innovative ways.
We just have to keep communicating our needs,
compromising our expectations
and being committed to each other and the baby.

Earth to Merri, earth to Merri. This is Nick speaking. Can you hear me? Can you hear me yet? I'm standing here shouting. What about me? What about my needs?

No one replies. No one was listening. It's all about Merri-and-the-baby. The baby-and-Merri.

What about my baby?

Nick@airspace.com.au — Anchorage, Alaska

For days I've been trying to say I want a say here. I've been trying to make plans. I think we need to make plans. If we're doing this, then we're doing it properly. Okay, no baby showers — let's not get tacky — but a flat together, somewhere. A parental dinner party to acknowledge we've hit a steep learning curve. Some organised childcare. A sense of the future.

And I say all this to her turned back, her glazed stare. Then she says, in her kindest voice, that she doesn't want to push me.

I need to push myself.

What Merri doesn't realise is how unreal the baby is to me, despite the ultrasound, the heart beat, the hospital visits. I can work away all night and forget its existence. I can go to classes, talk to my mates, fill in the footie tips, get on the Net and the baby fades to a slight nag at the back of my mind like the very beginning of a headache.

Don't you see, Merri? If I'm not pushed, I could walk away.

Maybe that's what you want. Maybe you want to do this by yourself. That's why you can't hear what I want. So I should just make my own plans, like Anchorage, Alaska? Leave you where you've wanted to be all along, in charge. You'll do it perfectly and with grace and I'll stop bumbling around, typically male, typically redundant.

Winter

We fight all weekend. The bungalow fills with our anger.
Winter's early this year.
Bare branches scrape across the roof
sounding like some animal trying to get in
to the warmth, but there's no warmth here.
Nick hunches over his laptop scowling.
My scissors flash dangerously.
We're playing the blame game.
If I hadn't been a little bit drunk.
If he'd had a condom in the glove box.
If we'd just waited the twenty-minute drive home.
It's too late. By five o'clock there's no light.
I tell him to go home anyway and he rides off,
muffled up in scarves and sweaters, doesn't even wave.
I stand and watch the bike lights wobble away.
My fingernails needle my palm.
Is this the way it ends? Something like a light
fading and both of us locking each other out
in the dark cold?

nick@airspace.com.au — This is how it ends

You pack up the clothes you had at her place, the one razor she hadn't used on her legs and the after-shave she bought you for a surprise and that nearly makes you cry but you don't because you've made your heart all steely, shiny and diamond-hard.

You say that you'll go with her to all the clinics. That the baby's yours as well and you want to be a good father. You want to be a better father than you ever had, but you're not sure how you'll manage it because he wasn't and so who'll teach you? You don't say all that, of course, because you can't. There's something blocking your throat. It could be a cold coming on.

It could be everything you haven't been able to say, just kind of balling up in a hard wad right where you have to speak and breathe and only certain words can sneak around and make their way out. Words like it's not my fault. Words like you care more about the baby than me. Words like I'm out of here. Little mean shrunken words.

The big words like love and want, like hold me and be with me, like I'm sorry and let's try again and be gentle with each other, just get stuck somewhere and never make it out into the silence.

She's sitting on the edge of the bed. Or she's lying on the bed with her back to your packing. She's not saying anything either. Her eyes are closed. Or they're open, staring at the wall. When you leave, you shut the door carefully behind you and pretend not to hear her crying.

Leigh's Journal — I'm stared at in the journo student's café

but not as I was when the news broke that I was on the
    shortlist.
Then it was enviously and people would saunter over
just to look at my filofax filling with appointments.
Now they're all pity and never-mind pats on my shoulder
until I growl, baring my teeth, scare them all back to
    their own seats.
No one's pitied me before, no one has ever felt sorry for
    me,
and they're not starting now.
I walk with my head high,
my face calm as a priestess.
I sit by myself in lectures,
in the library,
in tutorials.
I refuse all invitations and it works.
They stop coming.
They stop talking to me.
Let them call me arrogant.
I shut my ears.
I walk away from pity.
It has nothing to do with me.
What I want is a friend who'd get angry with me.
Someone to slam another tequila down
and curse the producers, the men in charge.
A friend to tell me about that guy who tried three times
and finally made it.

Someone to say it's a shit show anyway,
who needs it, and then toast to my success
next year.
I haven't made any friends since Merri.
Can't phone her, can't phone John.
I'll have to be my own best friend.
Shout myself another drink.
Wish myself the best of luck.
Tell myself I love me —
the words sounding stupid in my empty room.

Leigh's Journal — Second semester

Reassessed from ignominious Fail to
two Distinctions and one High Distinction.
And an invitation from a tutor to look at my Bali
    interview
and 'have a chat' about the Short Cuts experience,
particularly if I'm considering reapplying next year.
You bet!
I'm in her office faster than you can say
Take One,
clutching my video,
their reports on my work,
the folder of notes I've made
on all the Short Cuts programs,
my downloads from the Web,
my personal rants against Mitch's pathos,
Tang's earnestness, Jake's boyish charm
enchanced by expensive dental work, and
Thommo's full frontal attack (I'm a wild child and so
outrageously out there
you just have to love me).

She laughed at my baggage but she said
I had to try again. Listed my advantages this time
    round.
I'm already older. And I know my faults.
I've no heart, no compassion —
oh well, that'll be easy, won't it?
I'll just order some over the Net.

How many US dollars for a new heart,
a compassion graft?

Who dares reach in to wind up my clockwork heart
and start it thumping gladly?
They'd have to be stupid, mad or drunk.

The Dance

At the tail end of the party
after the people with kids had gone,
after Tammy had left with Lou Murphy and her son,
after the old forest campaigners went home to owl
    dreams
and the baker went straight to Dough,
after the couple from Melbourne took sleeping bags
    down by the dam
and Ruth's ex said a lingering good-bye
then revved his ute off in a cloud of hot exhaust
leaving six of us sitting round in the garden,
the talk drowsy and a little drunk,
someone changed the CD and
we're in that café on Sydney Road
on belly-dancing night.
Ruth swirls back into the light
wearing harem pants,
belly-button jewel,
bangles, a belt of silver coins
and a fringe pretending to be a top.
Oh yeah, the woman next to me murmured,
go Ruthie. And Ruth danced that first dance
for the music, for the night,
the wine, the stars,
for herself.
I couldn't stop watching.
The music lead her on
to lead us on, so sure of herself,

so strong. Then she danced for each of us,
winding us in tighter and tighter circles of bare
skin, her fingers extended like an invitation,
her belly slicked with sweat and kids' glitter.
I was on the end of the line, trying to be brave,
feeling drunk
and very horny.
She danced up to me,
little hip thrusts then a shimmy,
that made everything move
and all her silver sing and jingle.
On the drum solo fade-out, she held out her hands,
danced me straight into the house,
straight into her bedroom,
and I stood there
suddenly sober
as she took off her clothes.

Sex

Making love with Leigh
was like a song you'd once heard
that haunted you with snatches of melody
and a handful of words
you knew could change your life
if only you could remember them properly.
She was in my arms and then gone again.
Before Leigh, sex was fumbling under the blankets
hoping you were stroking or biting or whatever
the right thing and no one game to say.
Ruth pushed me on to her bed,
held back her dreads,
kissed me, put my hands where she wanted them,
laughed down at my dazed lust
and ...
when we got up late the next morning
the party had vanished
so we took our peanut butter toast back to bed
and learnt a little more about each other.

Of Real Estate and Romance

Lou Murphy buttonholes me as I'm putting out the new
    sci fi books,
catching me between Arthur C. and Phillip Dick.
'She's not as,' Lou pauses, pushes her hair away from her
    forehead —
even her hands look worried —
'self-contained as she seems.'
I'm feeling too jaunty:
'you mean, she's more your semi-detached?'
'She's more triple-fronted brick veneer,'
Lou hisses, 'if you get my nuclear family drift —
not that she'd admit that. And there's Tammy.'
'Lou,' I say, 'I know you think I'm a hard-living
city boy with a lot of bad trouble ganging up behind
    my back
and I hate to disappoint you,
but I think I'm just looking for love
like everyone else.'
We call a truce before moving on to True Crime.
She's not a happy camper, it's plain,
and so I warn Ruth that night and she laughs loudly,
drops the load of clean washing.
'She told me,' Ruth splutters, 'that you were sweet,
young and very vulnerable.'
Lou Murphy should stick to recommending book titles.

SEPTEMBER–
OCTOBER

Dad

Merri rings me at the bookshop.
Lunch hour, rush hour — four customers
and her voice wavering
as though she's talking through water.
She is crying
as she tries to tell me about our father's heart attack.
He is now in the Intensive Care Unit
doing okay but you can't be sure because
I can't hear anymore. My ears are ringing
as though her words were waves that have just dumped
    me
and now my mouth's full of sand
and I can't speak and someone, the guy who buys true
    crime,
is pushing me down in the chair.
Someone else is bringing me a glass of water
and I'm nodding and saying to someone —
I don't know who I'm talking to —
yes, yes, I'm okay,
yes, yes, I'll come straight away
and please, please tell him not to die,
tell him not
to die.

The Hospital

Ruth drives. I sit and jabber in the front.
At the first set of traffic lights she squeezes my leg.
That's all I remember of the drive,
Ruth's strong baker's hand on my leg.
She drops me at the hospital. Says she'll find a park,
she'll find me, just go and I do —
through the big glass doors of the hospital,
from the reception desk to the cardiac ward,
Room 24 and there's my father's bed
finally and my father,
smaller than he has ever been,
pinned to the bed by tubes,
his crumpled face grey against the hospital white.
Mum leaves him for the ten seconds it takes to hug me.
'John,' he says, sounding surprisingly like himself, 'you
      look great.'
I don't know what to say because he doesn't.
He looks as though he's given death the slip for a
      moment
but it will come back in the night,
any night, to claim him.
So I say nothing but take his hand,
the hand without tubes attached,
and I hold it in both my strong hands. He closes his
      eyes
and it is enough, to sit there with him
in this kind of silence
which is love even though neither of us say that.

I Didn't Know I Loved

I didn't know I loved
his voice crashing down like a surf beach,
his puns and professor's jokes,
the endless quotes from the classics,
his awkward back-slapping love
allowing itself one whiskey kiss
late on a Friday night.

I didn't know I loved
his habit of ceremony —
his way of telling how he cherished us,
the speeches at anniversaries,
his strings of Christmas lights,
the champagne brought out for every small triumph,
even my first shave,
as though by noting each of these with proper courtesy
he'd slow the moment down, have time to live it twice.

I didn't know I loved his knowledge
and how the rhythm of his learning,
the poetry and stories recited with awe and vigour,
had settled in my blood like some necessary chemical.

I didn't know him,
that big body collapsed
like a tranquillised beast,
his face thinned out and fearful.
My turn to sit and read to him,

the man who one whole summer
patiently read me my favourite books
over and over when I was too ill to keep the words
from staggering off their pages.

I didn't know how much of him I am
until this moment, picking up a book
and my voice with its own young energy and strength
filled the curtained space.

I didn't know how I loved him
until death caught his large wrist,
played tug-of-war,
and all of us, the rain outside, the winter trees,
even the oranges in a white bowl,
pulled him back,
back.

nick@airspace.com.au — Silences

Merri's dad has had a heart attack and I hear about it from John who is barely talking to me because of Merri. I can't talk to Merri. I can't visit the hospital. I can't see John or meet his new girlfriend. We exchange abrupt sentences on the phone, only just polite. I don't even ask to speak to Merri.

This isn't me. This is the me I'm scared of becoming.

My Father and My Daughter

I sit by my father's bed
in the cardiac ward
listening to the monitors beeping tiredly,
watching drugs dripping through the tubing,
hearing the coughing and soft steps of nurses,
their bullying, bright voices forcing cheer.
I place one of my father's hands on my belly
and we sit in silence waiting for the kick of new life.
My father's hand trembles
when my daughter's tiny limbs catapult him into love.

nick@haikuheaven.net.au — Free Renga; imagining her replies

Behind this old screen
the window frames grey clouds, rain
and cherry blossom.

My lap full of small clothes —
a scatter of spring colour.

Football crowds stagger home
flapping scarves and flags —
red and black drunks tumble down.

Each night the moon grows more round,
moon in the sky, moon in my bed.

I work all night, always cold,
stars chill company
after your voice, your warm arms.

The cat struts across late frost,
dark daisy prints in the ice.

I see you working, head bent
a lovely shadow.
I've crashed, data lost, blank screen.

Leigh's Journal — I saw Merri today in the quiet courtyard

where no one goes much this time of year.
She was hunched over on the cold park seat.
I would have turned round, walked away,
but I must have scuffled some leaves because she
    looked up.
Her face was all squished and red from crying.
I walked over — I was her friend once, right?
I said, Merri, it's not the baby is it?
I don't know why I thought of the baby first.
She shook her head and said 'Dad' and then blew her
    nose.
I sat down, put my arm around her,
and she told me about her father's heart attack,
she told me about arguing with Nick,
then she told me how much she hated me
and I said I was sorry. She asked me what for
and I said for everything — your father, Nick and
    mostly for John.
Then we hugged, awkwardly because of the baby.
And for the second time I asked her if we could be
    friends
but this time I meant for ever.

Friends

Not quite like old times, we meet each other
at cafes around the uni, shy with each other
polite, each leaving space for the other
to tell her story.

Not quite like old times, we go swimming together.
I admire her racing style.
She places her hand on my belly.
The kick catches her off-guard
and the change rooms echo with her laugh.

Not quite like old times, we discuss the future —
hers deliberately alone,
mine without Nick.
'Nick's mad,' she says, 'to let go of all this.'
And I find myself defending him,
making the excuses I wish he had made for himself.

Not quite like old times, we make a pledge of friendship
cautiously
don't shake on it but hug each other awkwardly
because of the baby
and everything else between us.

Reassessment

Dad has changed — it's not just that he's thinner
and quieter, he's also strangely more cheerful.
In the mornings he eats porridge with relish,
dreams over coffee and the newspaper,
talks about the morning sky, the quality of the weather.

When I get home from classes, he's weeding the garden
and whistling. Or reading a book in the cool spring air
or perhaps just sitting watching his garden grow.

After dinner together,
he and Mum sit for hours in the evenings, quietly
talking — reassessing. I look in and they're
side by side on the couch, holding hands.

I didn't know they were so coupled, still.
I thought — if I bothered — that they lived in
        separate worlds
and collided here, at home, accidentally.
Now I see, in the way he strokes her hair,
the tea she takes him in each morning before she
        leaves,
the way they're gentle with each other
in the face of his unreliable heart, just how
they're married and have been for twenty-five years.

And I see how Nick and I could have sat together
calmly united, each giving the other
time and space to reply to fears and uncertainties.
I rushed forward, catapulted into decision — too scared
to stay still in case they made me change my mind.
I dragged Nick with me — he just needed time.
If only I could go back, step back patiently, give him
     that time.
It's too late.

Leigh's Journal — Decisions

If I had the right subject I could make that
        documentary
with heart and compassion,
from the human of me
to you
if I cared.

And between one coffee and the next
I see it all so clearly.
Merri, her dark curls misted
with the spring drizzle, just waiting for my camera.
Not an in-your-face docco, but something like
conversation
close-focus
domestic and, if I can,
if I dared,
intimate.

Will she trust me?
Can I trust myself?
Intimate — a new word
I'm trying hard to learn.

Leigh's Journal — when Merri said yes

to me and my camera poking around
asking questions, filming the answers,
I made myself a deal.
I'm going to see Nick.
I'm going to try to talk reconciliation and sense
even though I know he hates me
and I'd hate me if I were Nick,
that bad bitch who dumped his best friend.
I'd slam the door right in my face.
I'm going in with no protective clothing
stripped down to heartache, mistakes
and the truth as a flag of surrender.
I'm going to tell him that he's missing
the chance of doing something big and wonderful
with someone you love.
I'm going in to tell him not to be like me.
Not to give up so easily. He's stronger than that.
He's better than that.

Leigh's Journal — I spent my lunch money

and bought a huge bunch of spring jonquils
smelling so sweet they make you sneeze.
I knocked at Nick's door, my face obscured by flowers.
I thrust them at his chest and pushed my way past him
right through to the kitchen.
You should have seen his face!
I talked at him.
I told him about Merri's secret tears,
how her new tough words
can't disguise how much she misses him.
I talked to him about the baby kicking.
I said, it's none of my business,
it's your life, but don't you think
you'll be missing out on the fun
if you walk away now and never look back?
Three hours, one packet of Tim Tams and two coffee
        pots later
I know he'll go back
with his heart in his hands
and I feel I've done something right
for once.

nick@airspace.com.au — Leopard-print leggings and second chances

I wait for her in the theatre car park. I don't lounge under a streetlight in my trench coat, smoking a cigarette like an old-fashioned movie star. I sit in my car, listening to Triple C on the radio. There's a bunch of flowers on the seat beside me. Tod, my American email buddy, recommended flowers. My mum recommended flowers. Leigh insisted on flowers. With the flowers is a small packet — a present for our baby. Mum helped me with the sizes but I chose the leopard-print leggings and matching hat myself.

I'm trying here, Merri. I'll keep trying.

Just give me a second chance.

Happily Ever After

We stumbled out — dress-rehearsal night —
after midnight and there, just like the movies,
under the brightest light in the car park
was Nick's old yellow car
and Nick beside it, hiding in a huge bunch of flowers.
Craig and Tan melted into the shadows
and I walked slowly towards those gerberas,
took them out of his hands
before they were squashed between us.
He mumbled my name into my neck
and I sighed his through his hair.

Nothing else needed to be said,
though we sat up until the small hours
saying it anyway: he'd been thinking of going to
        Anchorage,
he said, but Tod, his email friend,
isn't having his baby.
I was thinking of moving out of home
and in with Leigh, I tell him.
She's going to make a young-single-mum docco.
We're sort of friends again.
She got me off my arse,
he admitted, gave me a good talking to.

He stayed the night,
the baby kicking us both in the cramped bed.
We're going to celebrate being together again.
We're going to buy a queen-sized bed —
for the three of us.

NOVEMBER–DECEMBER

Ode to My Vegie Garden

Lift the jungle tangle to reveal
tomatoes
hanging like Christmas baubles,
so many
the plants bend towards the ground
whispering secrets to the basil,
all its fragrant leaves applauding
this hot summer, this evening rain.
The zucchinis listen slyly,
yellow flower trumpets cocked
for every green whisper.
That chilli-bush, caught red-fingering
the parsley — already gone to seed —
sets the snake beans' tongues waggling.
I sit outside braving the mosquitoes
to hear all my food growing
under the full moon.

Eight Months

I'm almost too big to sit at the sewing machine.
I lean forward over a moon-belly
they tell me holds a baby.
Sometimes I just don't believe it.
I look at babies in the street
and I know I'm not really having one of them —
even though I feel her kicking trying to get out.
My moon will surprise us all.
It will be a bunch of flowers or a perfect seashell.

I wait it out down in Costume.
Edie catches me napping when I should be sewing.
She covers for me. Gives me easy, dreaming jobs to do.
The last production of the year is a showcase for
        graduating students —
a surreal poetic drama set in the seventies in which
        ordinary people
find themselves stretched by extraordinary events.
I've read the program notes.
For us down here, it's mainly foraging and adjustments,
polyester and frocks.
Edie got the best pieces from a drag queen's garage sale.
(We cut up the fake fur coat
and made a poncho for the baby.)
One thing I think I've learnt this year is friendship,
the easy give and take, a comradely steadiness.
I have passed — even Movement Class —
that more out of sympathy than dexterity!

They want me back next year.
Even God said something nice
then warned about babies crying in his theatre.
It's all sorted. Dad's promised some childcare.
He reckons a baby's pace is what he needs. Life
        simplified
to feeds and sleeps and nappy changes.
It will give him time, he reckons, to grow his roses.
I've checked out the campus creche in case the nappies
        get him down.

I think we were cursed to live in interesting times —
it's been such a year of changes.
And the next one,
the one I'm waiting for with held breath,
the hugest of them all, my bunch of flowers,
my little shell,
my baby.

Nick@airspace.com.au — Secret Women's Business

We're counting down the weeks, the days. My bedside reading matter's changed from program manuals to birthing books. And still I know only one thing — the father never gets it right. I learnt that in the first antenatal class. I'm there to be sworn and screamed at, to get in the way, and not be where I'm needed at the exact second she wants me. I'm the chief tea-maker and brow-wiper and I'm not to expect any sympathy or attention. I'll probably faint in the middle or pass out at the end or not be able to cut the umbilical cord.

I know I won't be able to cut the umbilical cord.

Of course I want to be there. I wouldn't miss my daughter's birth for all Bill Gates' money.

Between you and me? It's secret women's business. I'd rather be pacing the waiting-room floor like in the old days, go in to kiss mother and baby when everything's cleaned up and it's all over except for the backslapping and champagne.

8th December

The midwife says it won't be long.
The baby's head is down where it should be.
Hours? Days?
She shrugs, pats my shoulder.
Have sex, she advises,
winking at Nick. Go for long walks.
Scrub the floor.
Keep calm.

Nick whispers secrets to the bulge
in my belly. He talks through my skin
to the baby within. He tells her jokes,
sings her songs. He listens,
he says, to her talking back.

I tell her, hurry up,
I'm counting the hours.
She wriggles around a little
as though she's getting comfortable,
as though she's settling in.
There's no room, I tell her. Look,
we've bought you a bassinette.
You'll be more comfortable there.
The sheets have rocking horses trotting over them.
John's made you a mobile.
Ruth's given you a dozen tie-dyed singlets.
Craig's sewn fuschia pink velour leggings for you.
Leigh's bought baby massage oil and your first hat.

We're all at the party waiting for the guest of honour.
Hurry up, girl. Stop growing your fingernails,
stop curling your hair. What do you mean you've
    nothing to wear?
I've scrubbed the floor. I walked my feet to blisters.
Your father's worn out.
Stop your teasing, little minx, and swim to us.
Swim.

9th December

Another blank day.
I sit around and drink tea.
Mum rings from work every thirty minutes.
Nick and I go for a long walk by the creek.
What's she doing in there I want to know.
Reading *War and Peace*?

It's like studying for an exam
they keep postponing.
Hey you, I've read the books — I know about
contractions, dilation, transition.
I know about breathing and panting,
about not pushing and then pushing.
I can spell perineum.
I need to see my toes again.

I've been so patient,
uncomplaining as trees,
while you grew yourself whole.
Now I yearn to see who we conceived
that party night in the car,
whose body I've fed with my own,
whose hands hold my heart
now and for ever.

10th December

I wake early. Can't sleep.
It takes me hours to choose what to wear
(as though there is much choice now I'm as big as a
    city).
All morning I'm restless.
I wish we were in a flat, Nick and I. I phone him.
We have to start looking for somewhere to live.
Come over, let's check out the classifieds.
He's here in no time, tells me I'm nesting.
I'm washing.
I'm washing her clothes
to make them all soft.
I'm hanging them in the sunshine
so they'll smell warm near her skin.
I'm counting my nappies like the days until Christmas.
And then it happens — a flicker of pain,
a mild cramp. I clutch Nick's hand.
It's started, I know.
And stupidly I want it to stop.
I want to go back to just being pregnant.
I'm not ready for this. I never will be.
It's all a mistake that we can't undo.
Nick's calling out to my Dad,
he's ringing the mothers.
I crawl back to bed,
pull up the covers. Nick holds me.
His grin is wide as the sky.
Dad makes tea and bad jokes nervously.

There's a girl in the mirror looking scared.
She doesn't know what she's taking on
she's just a kid,
kidding around,
playing at being a woman, pretending.
I'm sorry for her but I can't stop now.
When I see her next
she'll be older
they tell me, always tired, tied down
the rest of her life
stitched up.
Too late to cry now for the girl I'm leaving behind.
I slick on a bright smile instead,
count ten slowly, then,
I'm coming, my future,
ready or not.

Labour

The pain starts off like cramps
and I can breathe and talk through them.
Hours pass. I walk. Nick and I joke.
Mum comes home from work
to find us watching television with Dad.
I get up during the contractions, breathe.
The contractions come quicker, harder.
I stop talking through them.
We ring the hospital.
I hate the car.
I hate the hospital stairs.
I nearly hate the midwife.

The pain comes down like a pack of dogs.
I suck on the gas and float into their teeth.
I have never been so strong.
Nick holds my hand.
Mum wipes my forehead, tells me I'm a good girl.
The fanged dogs pant by my side.
Only they are real, their bloodied eyes nervous, wild.
I suck the gas again and they back away
until next time.
The dogs and I are running together.
I could go down on all fours like a bitch birthing.
I sway and rock to a moonsong only the dogs hear.
Someone is talking about pethedine but I'm not
    listening.
They say I'm tired but I'm sledding along with the dogs.

They're pulling and dragging. They won't let me go
    under.
Then the pain changes, burning. I have to push.
I have to push but they tell me to pant and I do, I do
until I can't. I shake my head dumbly.
I'm handed a mirror, shown a head
down there between my legs.
I don't believe it's a baby but I push down,
down further still,
until there's a slither of shoulders —
she's out
wailing in the new air.

nick@airspace.com.au — Birth Announcement

At 12.12 this morning, after an eight-hour labour, my daughter was born. 3015 grams and 50 centimetres long from the top of her silvery head to her ten perfect toes. I'm awestruck, gobsmacked, speechless at her beauty. Her tiny hand latches on to my finger and my heart somersaults. Her eyes open and it's the dawn of an unchartered day. She yawns and I look up to see Merri's dazzled face and know I look just as foolishly in love.

Bring on the cigars, the champagne. I want everyone to know. I want the PCs of the world to flash this message on to everyone's screen. I want fireworks and a public holiday declared. I want a meteor shower. I want the earth to pause before it resumes its orbit.

I want to keep her safe for ever and ever.

Saying Hello to My Niece

Merri phones to say she's started labour and Ruth and I
    drive down.
We check in at the hospital; so different from last time
when we'd batted down the highway, death on our
    minds.
Mum gives us both a distracted hug —
she's Merri's other support person —
and then orders us to take Dad to dinner.

We walk up the road where Carlton's buzzing.
And even though we're all keyed up, waiting
for Dad's phone to ring, we catch the summer zing,
loiter in front of the menus displayed in windows,
listen to the spruiking maître'd's on the pavement
and after dinner we browse for a while,
guiltily, in the bookshops and Dad buys
The Oxford Treasury of Children's Verse
and gets them to giftwrap it.

Back in the waiting room we drink cups of tea.
Ruth chats to the midwives in her easy, country way.
Dad and I do the cryptic crossword.
We drink more tea.

At about midnight I go up the corridor to have a pee
and hear a woman groaning, a guttural animal sound
that stops me like a punch — it's almost sexual
that noise, despite the pain that caused it.

When I realise it's Merri, I feel like a voyeur.
Minutes later a midwife calls us in and there they are —
the new family — my sister, Nick and their daughter —
her small, scrunched-up face unbelievably beautiful.

Dad proffers the giftwrapped book. We cry and laugh.
I kiss my niece, hug Merri and Nick, look at Ruth
who looks back with her steady eyes.
Later, I'll ask her how she felt —
did it make her want another baby?
I'm not building dream castles.
I like where I am now:
saying hello to my niece,
helping Dad pour champagne,
listening to Mum talking nonstop,
watching my girlfriend's long fingers
as she strokes the baby's head.
I'm learning to stay here
relishing the moment
before moving on.

Leigh's Journal — She's twelve hours old

the first time I see her, but she looks as though
she's got the world sussed. I'm almost too scared
to hold her but Nick makes me sit down,
shows me how to support her head,
and for all of five minutes she's in my arms.
Then she screams for her mother and I hand her over
quick smart.

For hours, though, I kept smelling her,
that milky-sweet baby smell.
I'm glad we're friends again,
Merri and I. I know she's wary,
doesn't want me getting too close.
There's a barrier there. I'll be good
with the baby, I'll be the single friend
always ready to wheel the pram to the playground,
always on hand for last-minute babysitting,
the ever-helpful guest, tasting their domestic bliss.
Learning.

Christmas Lilies

We were going to call her Rose or Norah,
an old-fashioned name for a twenty-first century girl,
but when she arrived she was wearing Nick's fair skin,
his grey eyes and there was pale down on her head —
so soft I couldn't help licking it
as though she was my pup.
The names we'd chosen were tawny and pink,
our girl's silvery, luminous as a star.
Mum brought in a huge bunch of Christmas lilies —
their heady fragrance overwhelming the room's blood
      smell.
You always know it's Christmas when the lilies bloom
so tall on their single strong stems.
I looked down at my new bloom
and Nick and I named her right then —
a liquid lilt of sound.
May she grow like those flowers,
matching her beauty with unwavering strength,
and may she forgive us all our young mistakes.
Welcome to the world, light of my heart,
new girl-child,
welcome home, Lily.

Leigh's Journal — It had to happen

we had to meet sooner or later.
I'm glad to get it over with —
the reddened confusion,
my slightly erratic heartbeat,
the stammering greetings
and not knowing where to look
or who to look at — him or his girlfriend.

Sure it hurt, seeing him again
and not alone, but it's done now.
We can move on.
I dream that one night
years in the future
we'll get pissed together
and I'll tell him I had to do it —
and I'll tell him that if I hadn't
he'd never have ended up wherever he is
— married to a country hippy, probably,
with four kids sprawled on an old couch
watching telly while the vegies take over the backyard.
I didn't belong, I'll say, and we'll agree,
raising a toast to each other and the lives that we've
        found.
Then I'll turn on my cell phone,
jump in my car, cruise down the highway
back to the real world.

I'm making it up, of course.
Maybe we'll never again get drunk together,
never talk easily, but I like that scene.
I like who I am when I play it over in my head.
It makes my heart easier,
imagining us ending like that,
as though that was always the way
it was meant to be.

JANUARY

Leigh's Journal — New Year's Eve with the M & M's

is home-delivered haute cuisine from the Thai place
that has four chef's hats awards, and
two bottles of Veuve — we know it's French,
sweetie, but the local stuff — well,
and Marina's eloquent, elegant bare shoulders
undressed by somewhere chic that's seen in *Vogue*
shrug helplessly.
We're watching the fireworks on our new flat-screen tv.
No overseas jaunt this year.

I'd rather be anywhere else but no one asked.
Merri carefully explained, in the sort of phone call
you'd rather not have answered, the impossibility of me
      crashing
their Daylesford trip and I agreed.
I'd rather be here, fishing for chili calamari
with Marina's antique ivory chopsticks
(don't think about the elephants!),
than up there playing aunt to all that family.
And imagining how it is between them,
John and his dreadlocked girl.

Moving on will be easier when there's a place on the
    map marked
with an X that's mine. Then I'll play charming remorse
and give plain jealousy the shove.
For now it's another glass of Veuve, thanks Mum,
and here's to a year which treats me better.

Preparing New Year's Eve

We're having a family party — Merri, Nick and Lily,
Ruth, Tammy and me. Tammy's made popcorn strings,
crepe paper streamers and a banner which says
Happy New Year!
in wobbles and blobs.
There's a chocolate cake with hundreds and thousands
and marshmallows to toast on the barbie.
And Tammy's wrapped presents for everyone
under the New Year tree.
I have mine already — she's in the garden
picking roses, baseball cap jammed over her dreads.
The year's trooped through all its seasons.
I've gone from heartbreak to
heartwhole and grateful
to whatever forces steered me here —
this calm place where the future is another picnic,
another child's piggy-back ride,
another coffee at The Harvest,
and who knows, maybe this time next year
Ruth and I will be gathering our tomatoes from our
        vegie garden,
maybe my catamaran plan will be blutacked on our
        bedroom wall
and each morning Tammy will wake us with her morning
        news.

For the moment, good enough to simply be here
like part of the furniture, Ruth's lover,
Tammy's favourite story-reader,
and enjoy the last hours of this old year
as the day warms up and the beer gets colder.

New Year's Eve

We get an early start, or try to —
so many little things to remember:
nappies, spare gro-suits, nighties,
the tiniest bonnet
and little pairs of socks.
And then we have to stop every five minutes
to blurt Lily's tummy
or hold on to one of her hands
or just stare at her beauty.
She has to be fed
and changed and changed
and fed again.
We'll never get there.

We do — after an anxious hour on the highway
checking Lily all the time,
and then half an hour finding Ruth's house
from the scratchy map John sent.

Unpack the car, change Lily,
feed her and slowly unwind.
Good food smells in the kitchen.
Ruth takes Lily and Tammy takes my hand,
shows me around.
In the kitchen Nick and John open a beer
and settle down for some serious men's talk.
Ruth puts an umbrella up by the dam and we watch
    Tammy

dog-paddling, watch Lily burping, watch the last day
of the old year slide into afternoon and then evening.
Wishes for the New Year?
Oh, just more of this —
a slow year, baby-paced,
a year of quiet love.

Nick@airspace.com.au — New Year's Eve

The barbecue's at just the right temperature, the steak and sausages are smoking. Ruth's tofu is safe from animal fat contamination, Tammy's pineapple rings are browning. Swigging my beer I feel like a man in charge. I am a man in charge. I'm a father, qualified for this serious barbecue thing.

I'm a father. Still scares me. I look at her little face and just pray I won't ever see it look back at me in fear or horror or even drooped with disappointment at a soccer game forgotten, a swimming lesson ditched for a session at the pub. She's taught me already how my father wielded his power and will and it was never, never my fault. She's taught me how my mother worked for years to heal those wounds, her inexhaustible love a balm.

I can only say I love you because my mother said it all those years when he couldn't. And when she gave up on him and left his dark moods, his binges, his self-hatred, she kept saying it for both of us, even when I screamed with all my thirteen-year-old fury, she said it and believed.

Lighten up boyo, it's a party night and Merri's waving her glass at me to fill and Lily's waving her feet, just because she can, and John puts an arm around my shoulders and together we look at all the unexpected beauty that's dropped into our open hands.

Happy New Year!